FRED

KAILA EUNHYE SEO

Peter Pauper Press, Inc.
White Plains, New York

For my loving mother, Jungbok Lee,
and awesome sister, Jihye Seo

Published by Peter Pauper Press, Inc.
202 Mamaroneck Avenue
White Plains, New York 10601
U.S.A.

Published in the United Kingdom and Europe by
Peter Pauper Press, Inc.
c/o White Pebble International
Unit 2, Plot 11 Terminus Road
Chichester, West Sussex PO19 8TX, UK

Designed by Heather Zschock

Library of Congress Cataloging-in-Publication Data

Seo, Kaila Eunhye, author, illustrator.
Fred / Kaila Eunhye Seo. -- First edition.
pages cm
Summary: "Fred is a young boy whose world is filled with magical,
colorful friends that fill his heart with joy. However, as he gets older things
start to change and these childhood friends slowly fade away until he
can no longer see them. But a chance meeting with a special young girl
reminds Fred that magic and wonder never really disappear...they live
forever in our hearts"-- Provided by publisher.
ISBN 978-1-4413-1731-5 (hardcover : alk. paper) [1. Imaginary
playmates--Fiction. 2. Friendship--Fiction.] I. Title.
PZ7.1.S46Fr 2015
[E]--dc23
                                                    2014029032

ISBN 978-1-4413-1731-5
Manufactured for Peter Pauper Press, Inc.
Printed in Hong Kong

7 6 5 4 3 2 1

Visit us at www.peterpauper.com

In a small town, there was a boy quite different from everyone else.

His name was Fred.

He was able to see and
believe in things . . .

. . . that others could not.

He saw them roam here and there all throughout the town, in all different shapes and sizes—from big and little, to round and square.

Sometimes they acted like the wind and
moved branches out of the way for people.

And sometimes they acted like shade and kept people cool on hot summer days.

Best of all, they were like a playground.
Fred would swing, slide, and jump!

He loved playing with his friends and Fred never felt alone when he was with them.

People often looked at Fred like he was strange.

But he didn't care, because he was happiest
when he was with his friends.

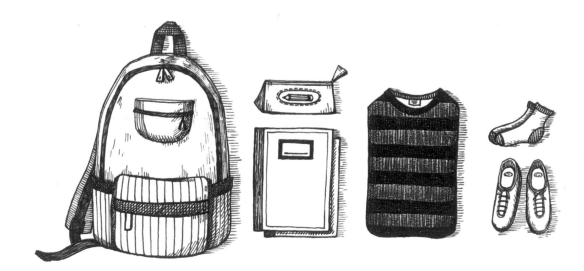

Until one day when things changed.

Fred's mother walked him into town for his first day of school.
There were lots of other children—all the same age as Fred.

His teacher was very nice.
She read them stories and
gave them snacks.

At the end of the day, Fred's
mother came to pick him up.
He was so excited!

He told her about everything he
did in his new school . . .

. . . with his new friends.

When he and his mother got home,
Fred ran up to his room and dropped
off his backpack.

"Hi Fred! Wanna play outside?" his friends asked.

"Sorry guys. I can't play right now.
I'm going to my friend Peter's house," Fred replied.

"I'll see you guys later!"

But "later" came and went.

First one day,

then another,

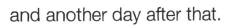

and another day after that.

As time went by, Fred grew older.
And as he made new friends,
he forgot about his old friends,
and he didn't see them anymore—
just like everyone else.

The years passed by and Fred did things that older people often do. He went to work.

He drank coffee.

He ate the same things everyday for breakfast, lunch, and dinner, and then he went to sleep.

He lived each day very much like the day before.

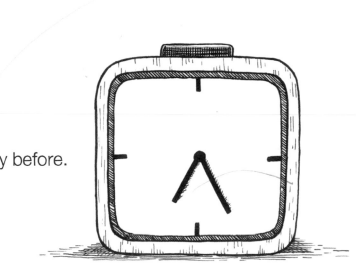

Some days he would go to the park
where he used to play as a child.

He would sit in the shade and
wonder why he sometimes
felt empty and alone.

One day as Fred sat in the park reading a book,
he looked up and saw a little girl staring at him.

"Would you and your friends like a lollipop?" the girl asked.
"Excuse me?" said Fred.

"Here. Strawberry lemon is my favorite,"
said the girl.
Before Fred could respond, she turned
and continued on her way.

Her words kept circling in Fred's head—around and around and around.

Slowly a light began to fill his heart—
the part of his heart that had been
dark for a long time.

He never had been.

And he knew he was not alone after all.